The Tale of Despereaux™

THE GRAPHIC NOVEL

Adapted and illustrated by
MATT SMITH *and* DAVID TILTON

Based on the motion picture screenplay

Based on the book by KATE DiCAMILLO

CANDLEWICK PRESS

First paperback edition 2008

Library of Congress Cataloging-in-Publication Data is available.

Library of Congress Catalog Card Number 2008932000

ISBN 978-0-7636-4075-0 (paperback)

2 4 6 8 10 9 7 5 3 1

Printed in the United States of America

This book was typeset in Formal 436.
The illustrations were digitally created.

Candlewick Press
99 Dover Street
Somerville, Massachusetts 02144

visit us at www.candlewick.com

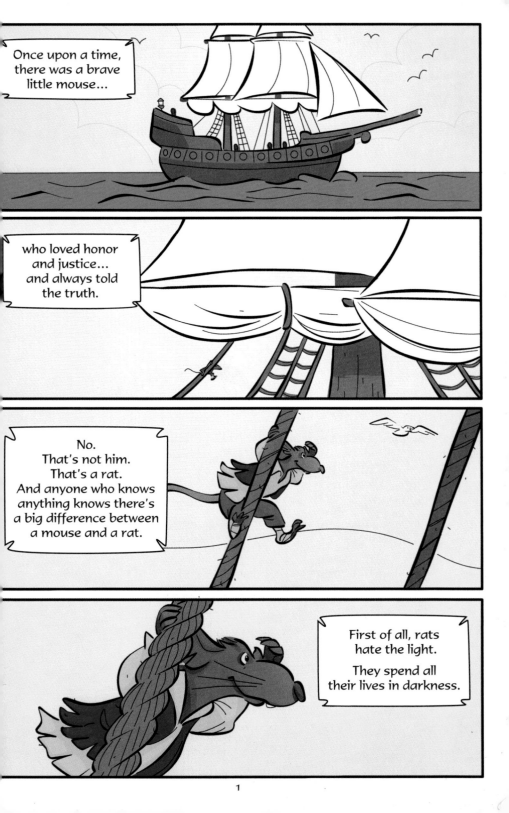

They're also terrified of people, which is why they slink and cower all the time.

BOINK!

BOINK!

Sigh.

Tell me that thing again, please. Just once more, I promise!

Fine.

"We are headed to Dor. One of the most magical places in the whole world."

That is *not* what you said before.

You said, "Every place we go has something special about it, and in Dor it's soup."

See? You know it!

In Dor, Christmas was nothing. Well, they still celebrated it, but it was nothing compared to...

On the first Sunday of every spring, Dorians young and old would flock toward the castle...

to hear the official royal soup announced.

Deep within the castle kitchen, Chef André and his staff were busily putting the final touches on that year's creation.

But things weren't going quite as planned.

More Onions!

How many times do I have to say it?

More onions, more onions, more ONIONS!

Gulp!

The townspeople would gather in the square, awaiting the king's announcement, and as the aroma filled the air...

they would begin to speculate as to the contents.

C'mon, me lovelies! Place your bets!

It's a bisque! 2 to 1!

In fact, the suspense was killing them. And in many ways, that was their favorite part.

And Roscuro the rat was just as excited as everyone else.

Welcome, friends of soup.

And now, the moment you've all been waiting for...

Princess Pea, the envelope, please.

Thank you, sweetie.

HURRAH!

It is my pleasure to announce this year's royal creation from...

Now, a big part of being a genius is making everyone *believe* that you are.

And sometimes that takes a little help.

There are all kinds of genies. Some are in lamps...

some are in bottles...

but, of course, where else would a soup genie be but in a cookbook?

FZZZT!

POOF!

Roscuro found his way to the dining hall, where the royal family awaited the first taste of Chef André's soup.

Voilà!

This smells amazing!

15

It moved!

It moved?

My soup MOVED!

No, it did not move.

It moved!

Cough!

Oh, Your Highness—

AHHHHHH!

A RAT! THERE IS A RAT IN MY SOUP!

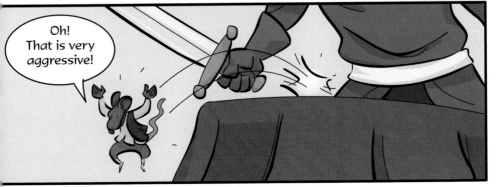

He's going into the kitchen!

Over there!

Clack!

Clack!

Clack!

Get him!

He's cornered!

SWIPE!

Yikes!

SLASH!

CLANG!

EEEEE!

Har! Got 'im!

And Roscuro fell...

into the abyss!

You don't need to be afraid.

Who—who are you?

I know it's dark, but you'll get used to it.

Just a rat like you.

After that most unfortunate day, the family gathered to pay its respects.

Today we lay to rest the Queen of Dor...

You may not feel it often, but when you do, grief is the strongest thing that a person can feel.

And death can feel so unfair, as if someone has taken something from you.

When something hurts this much, you think there must be a reason.

There must be someone to blame.

So think about this: what happens when you make something illegal that is just a natural part of the world?

You may as well make flies illegal... or sweat...or Monday morning.

But that's just what the king did—

out of a terrible sadness.

Sunlight left, and the world went gray.

Soup kettles piled up in the gutter...

as colors faded into one another, and dark clouds filled the sky.

For a long time, it wouldn't rain.

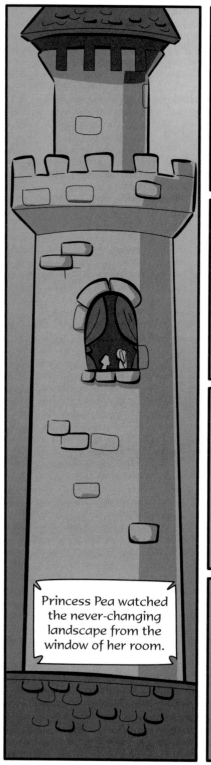

Princess Pea watched the never-changing landscape from the window of her room.

I wish it would rain, Louise.

You an' the whole world, madam.

Now, stay still. Almost finished fixin' your lovely dress.

Louise, do you think there's a bit of light somewhere in the world?

Dunno, ma'am.

I think there is. You just need to know where to find it.

Remember how this started "Once upon a time there was a brave little mouse...."? Well, if you know anything about fairy tales, you know that a hero doesn't appear until the world really needs one...

Pardon! Excuse me!

and sometimes he or she appears in the most unlikely of places.

Oh, excuse me!

Lester Tilling?

Oh, Mr. Mayor!

Where are you going?

Oh... well...my baby is having a... I mean my wife is having a...

Oh, right. Congratulations.

28

But he isn't cowering! He's looking right at us!

Oh, don't worry! He'll learn to cower!

They all do in time.

But what if he doesn't?

Mom, he's so puny!

And look at those ears!

And from the very beginning, Despereaux Tilling heard more, saw more, and experienced more than any of the other mice.

Several months later...

Despereaux, don't do it!

It's too dangerous!

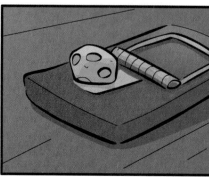

Spring

SNAP!

Despereaux Tilling had no idea he was small—smaller than all the other mice.

In his own mind, Despereaux was a GIANT!

and Mrs. Tilling met with espereaux's teacher to discuss his behavior....

We're worried about him.

He doesn't scurry. He doesn't cower. At first we thought he would grow out of it, but...

Some kids are slower than others. He'll cower in time. We'll work on it.

Yes, but—

It'll be fine. I promise.

You can send in your son now.

Later, on the outskirts of own, Despereaux approached an iron grate....

Despereaux, what are you doing?

We're not even s'posed to be here. That's the dungeon!

There are rats down there!

They'll eat you!

And pull your arms off!

How far down is it?

I don't know. No one has ever come back!

How come?

'Cause that's where you go when you break the rules...

when you get— when you get b-b-b-b-banished!

Despereaux crawled out onto the long plank that hung over the grate.

He-llo-o!

He-llo-o...

He-llo-o...

Despereaux's call echoed in the darkness of the void below.

Far off in the gloom, a horrible singing filled the air...

Stinky, dark and foul and rotting, oozing sores and blood that's clotting. Mmm! Delicious! Hits the spot! It's great to be a rat!

When we see a chained-up victim, our hearts bleed—and then we lick him. Chew his ears and nose—THEY picked him. We're just being rats!

Give us flesh and filth and bile.

What you think is gross and vile...

makes us sing and dance and smile.

We like to live like that!

The rats all danced and sang, except one—Roscuro.

You're not dancing.

No, you weren't.

Oh, I was!

Well... I'm just... watching.

We'll, that's not very grateful of you. After I've taken you under my wing...

Roscuro hurried away from the other rats. Botticelli was right; Roscuro was missing something.

He glanced in either direction as he reached his secret hiding place, a chink in the masonry of the stone wall.

a narrow shaft of light.

It was nothing but a small crevice in the castle's construction, but from there Roscuro could see...

It was very faint, but Roscuro basked in the dim glow of the small beam.

His friends just didn't seem to understand him...

He is so weird!

No kidding!

In a very different part of the castle, Despereaux stared up at the light from the storeroom window...

feeling that there just had to be something more out there...

and maybe even someone more like him.

and Mr. and Mrs. Tilling were still concerned about their son's unmouselike behavior.

You coddle that boy that's the problem!

He is so little. I had to help him!

He is not going to be afraid unless you allow him to be afraid!

His brother, Furlough, will teach him.

Despereaux, do what Furlough does.

And don't do anything he doesn't!

Later that day, at the Tilling household...

And if he's afraid of something—

Then you need to be afraid of it, too!

All right, we're going to head to the library.

I'm going to show you how to eat books.

OK, are you ready?

YEAH!

Come on, Furlough!

Hurry up!

The Royal Library

You start by nibbling along the edge of the page....The glue is all right, but it's the pages that taste best.

You're not supposed to *read* it! You're supposed to *eat* it!

Once upon a time...

Ooooh, that sounds great!

OK, I'll come back in an hour.

And no reading! It's a rule!

As soon as Furlough was gone, Despereaux turned his attention back to the story....

But in a cruel and frightened world, men like that were scarce indeed.

For it wasn't just courage that made a knight...

and it wasn't just chivalry, either.

In this world built on courage and chivalry and honor, knights pledged their lives to fight for truth, to defend the weak, to seek justice, and to always—

The spell of the story was suddenly broken by the sound of music from somewhere nearby....

Despereaux followed the music down a long hallway.

He listened as the same sad refrain was played over and over.

Princess Pea was also listening to her father playing his mournful song.

Pea returned to her chamber, not knowing that she was being followed by a tiny mouse.

Then she turned away, saddened, for the king was lost in grief and would not leave his room.

With tears streaming down her cheeks, Princess Pea stared out into the ever-cloudy sky.

Why are you crying?

Um... down here.

AHHH! Are you a rat?

No.

44

But "longing is just love waiting to be born."

You're a strange little mouse.

Thank you.

The princess reached down to offer her hand....

Where did you hear that? About "longing"?

In a story.

A story? About what?

About a beautiful princess like you. In a castle like this.

46

HA-HAAA!

As Despereaux flew down the hallway in pure bliss, he didn't notice the servant scrubbing the floor on her hands and knees.

Now, there are all kinds of princesses: some are born that way, some marry into it, and some are destined to be princesses only in their own minds...

but at one time or another, almost every little girl longs to be a princess.

And Miggery Sow was no exception. She had always wanted to be a princess, even when she lived back on Uncle Ned's farm.

Before she came to the castle, Mig had spent most of her time on the farm with the pigs: feeding them, cleaning up after them, and talking to them....

Yup. I'm gonna live in that castle someday.

OINK!

OINK!

OINK!

I'm gonna live right there.

OINK!

Right up near the tippy-top!

SNORT!

Ah, quit your daydreaming!

AND FEED THOSE SWINE!

Uncle Ned screamed at poor Mig most of the time...so much that she didn't always hear things clearly....

Yes, I know. And it's going to be all mine.

No, you deaf little urchin! I said, "Feed those swine!"

Grrrr!

Mig's father had left her with Ned when was just a little girl. So for as long as she could remember, it had just been Mig and the pigs.

But that turned out all right, because she got along with them quite nicely.

That's right... I'm gonna have a special room just for me dresses, an' another for me knickers.

OINK!

SQUEE!

One day a man from the castle came to buy pigs from Ned, as he often did. Only this time the man was looking for a servant as well.

Twenty for the big ones, fifteen for the sow...

and twelve for the girl.

Fifteen for the girl.

Same as the sow.

And so that day, Miggery Sow found herself on her way to the castle.

I told ya!

Oink!

Sometimes it doesn't take much to think your dreams have come true....

I told ya I'd make it to the castle!

OOOO-EEE!

Even though Mig lived in the castle now, it wasn't at the tippy-top, and there was no special room for her dresses, so still she longed for the life of a princess.

Back at the Tilling home...

She was beautiful.

Like an angel.

You're crazy!

And she smelled so amazing!

Like a garden.

Despereaux, you can't talk to a *human*! That's the worst thing you can do!

No, it's the best thing I ever did!

Sssshhhhh! If anyone ever finds out, you'll be thrown in the dungeon!

What's going on in here? What's all this about talking to humans?

Uh-oh!

Furlough, I want to see you in my study... right now!

...Are you sure?

A real human?

A princess?

That's what he said!

We need to tell them. We need to tell the Mouse Council.

But they will send him to the dungeon!

He'll get eaten by rats!

Not if we beg... if we really beg...and show them that he's changed...

that he's afraid... that he's afraid and he's turned into a real mouse.

I'll go get him. Better we get to the council before they hear about it.

Despereaux!

Where is he?

Back at the library, Despereaux delved back into the story...for himself— and for the princess!

But what he didn't know was that he had been followed...

DESPEREAUX TILLING!

by the Mouse Council!

How long have you been working on this book?

Um... a week?

A week? You've hardly started it.

Well...I was... I just wanted to see how it ends.

Despereaux was brought before the Mouse Council to hear the charges against him.

...Refused training as a mouse, refused to respect the will and guidance of elder mice, repeatedly engaged in bold and unmeek behavior...

had personal contact with...

a human being!

Despereaux Tilling, are these charges true?

Yes. I think so.

Do you understand the penalty for associating or conversing with a human being?

Despereaux glanced around the courtroom. It was perhaps the first time he had ever felt afraid....

Lester...

Back at the Tilling home, Lester and Antoinette fretted about the fate of their son....

Isn't there something you can do?

Antoinette, stop.

You have to trust them. They're the council... 'cause...

'cause they're the council.

Is there anything you wish to say in your defense?

Well...
it was a very
good story,
and...

she was a
very beautiful
princess....

Despereaux Tilling,
the judgment of this
court is not an easy one,
but it is clear.

Our laws are
here to protect us and
our way of life. And when
one of our citizens strays
from our way
of life...

he becomes
a threat to
us all.

It is the
judgment of this
court that you should be...
banished...from these
walls forever.

You shall be
remanded into the
custody of Hovis the
Threadmaster...

who will prepare you for your descent into the unknown world. You shall be exiled—alone—into the dungeons of Dor...

from which no house and no light has ever escaped.

Hovis the Threadmaster emerged from the shadows....

So you're the "brave" one.

I guess.

That's good. It'll carry well down there.

Hovis unraveled a length of thread from the spool he carried.

Wear this proudly. There's no shame.

Hovis and Despereaux left the crowd behind as they walked toward the boundaries of the mouse world.

It's all right.

They're too scared to come down here.

Finally they reached their destination....

In there?

I'm afraid so.

Despereaux hurtled into the abyss.

WHIRRRRR!

BONK!

BONK!

THUMP!

Despereaux untied the thread and left it behind as he turned toward the darkness. He jumped back quickly, startled by the shape looming beside him — the skull of an unlucky prisoner.

Hello? Hello?

Gregory the jailer answered.

Who is that?

Who goes there?

64

65

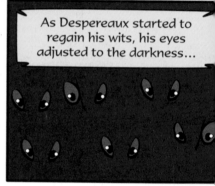

Thrown into a pipe by the mob of rats, Despereaux tumbled out onto a hard stone floor...

Mouse!

Mouse!

Mouse!

Mouse!

Mouse!

into what appeared to be a massive arena. He looked up to see hundreds of rats— jeering and chanting at him!

Good crowd, ain't it, sir?

Yes...

It is, quite.

C'mon! Let's go, buster!

Yeah, lick 'em clean!

Eat every bone!

That's it, that's it. Keep moving.

Roscuro lowered his voice to a whisper as they left the roaring crowd behind.

It's OK. Keep walking.

Right up there.

Keep walking....

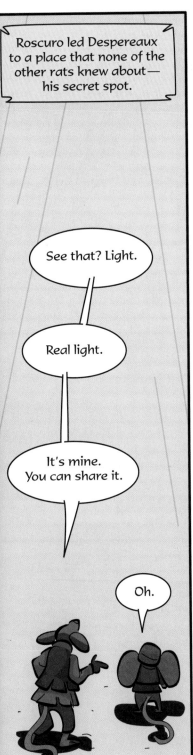

Roscuro led Despereaux to a place that none of the other rats knew about— his secret spot.

See that? Light.

Real light.

It's mine. You can share it.

Oh.

It isn't much.

But there isn't much anywhere since the world turned gray.

You're not going to eat me?

I don't eat mice.

Then what do you eat?

Over the next few weeks, Despereaux told Roscuro everything he knew about loyalty and honor and chivalry and courage. He told him about the princess and where her longing came from—that she missed the rain and the soup and even the rats....

Even the rats?

He told him about the code of honor. About his noble quest. About duty and loyalty. And there in the darkness of the dungeon...

two "knights" pledged devotion to a princess who was trapped inside a castle...

trapped in a life full of pain and longing.

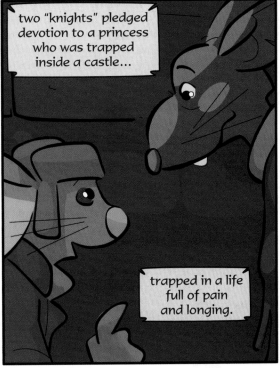

Please, take it away.

Very well, ma'am.

In the servants' quarters, Mig stared into her mirror....

Princess? Who's the princess? I'm a princess.

I'm the princess....

Later.

Gor! She's the princess, an' I have to carry the sloppy, gloppy, stinky food down into the damp, dark, dingy...

A person could get lost forever down here.

Mig stumbled in the dark until she found a small circle of light.

Din-din.

Slop.

How am I s'posed to eat this swill?

Gor! Stop that!

I don't have to put up with all this!

I serve the princess!

Well, I don't want to hear it. Had me own little princess once, and now I don't.

Gor! You had a princess?

Yeah... every dad's got a princess... till he stops being a dad, of course.

And so Mig brought the empty bowls back up to the kitchen....

Every day, back up the stairs, out of the dungeon, and up into the castle.

And Roscuro saw a way up and a way to change everything.

Roscuro decided to tell Despereaux about the quest he planned to undertake.

What kind of quest?

To right a terrible wrong.

But who did you wrong?

OK. You know how they banished the rats?

Sure...yes.

Well, it wasn't all the rats they banished. I mean, they did...

but it was because of one rat in particular.

Oh.

And so the next time Mig returned to the kitchen with the empty dishes, she also took along something extra...

something Mig could not see hidden under the napkin. Something small yet determined...

something—or someone—on a noble quest to set his wrongs to right!

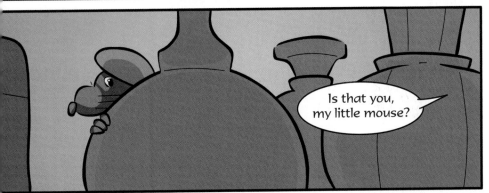

AHHHH!
A RAT!

No, no!

In fear, Pea seized a poker and swung it wildly at Roscuro!

SWOOOOSH!

BAM!

EEEE!

It's a RAAAAAAT!

As Roscuro fled into the hallway, the palace guards scrambled into action, responding to Pea's cries!

The only escape was out the window...

Halt! Halt! You there, rat!

and into a free fall!

Far below, Roscuro saw his only hope rushing up toward him....

Pulling himself up, Roscuro peered into the window of a darkened storeroom.

In the cluttered broom closet, Roscuro wandered aimlessly toward an empty pail.

He caught his reflection in the curved and pitted surface. He looked mottled and grotesque.

How would YOU feel if your own name was a bad word?

Well, that's how Roscuro felt about who he was—a rat.

When your heart breaks, it can grow back crooked. It can grow back twisted, gnarled, and hard.

Roscuro still had "longing," but now he just longed for someone whose heart was hardened...

whose heart had grown back crooked like his....

Pretty princess.

Pretty princess pie.

Miggery Sow was too fixated on her thoughts to notice a small visitor enter the room.

What a pretty princess.

Should be my jewel-y, girl-y hat...

all sitting on my pretty princess head.

SHHRRIIKK!

Down in the kitchen...

CLINK! CLANK!

Huh?

a sleepy chef André is awakened by a noise.

'Allo?

What are you doing?

Um... I need this for a baby.

No! Not for a baby. For "milady."

I mean for milady. To chop her some apples!

Now turn and leave.

Mig wrapped the knife in a towel and left.

Hurt is a funny thing. The same thing that makes one person angry can make another person sad.

Many years earlier...

Ned, take care of my little princess....

I can't no more.

Oh, aye, Gregory. I will.

Don't worry.

I'm sorry. So, so sorry.

When the blanket slipped, a heart-shaped birthmark was revealed on the little girl. Gregory always said she had too much heart...

But let's face it. It's hard to see something on your back. In fact, you can have a good heart and not even know it.

You can do this. You know you can.

I know I can.

and that's why they had to put some of it on the outside.

She belongs in the dungeon. And you belong in the palace. Like a princess.

Like a princess.

Mig! What are you doing?

Cleaning, ma'am.

With rope? You look ridiculous.

And at those words, Mig turned a deep red.

Minutes later, Mig marched her prisoner down into the dungeon's depths.

You can't do this, Mig.

Gor...seems I am, ma'am.

You'll get into a terrible amou of trouble.

Don't listen. You're the princess now.

I'm the princess now.

You can't do this to me!

Help! Help!

It's no use, ma'am. No one can hear you.

HELP!

Ah, but someone can.

Wrapping himself in a discarded cloak...

Despereaux sets out toward the cry for help.

Moving disguised through a throng of rats, he follows the sound to...

a prison cell!

HELP! HELP!

Despereaux pulls back the brick that conceals the lighted shaft.

He drops down...

into a pile of soot...

and emerges covered head to toe in white dust!

Despereaux's only hope is to escape up the chimney shaft.

Despereaux reaches the top...

but another challenge awaits our hero.

Traps.

Lots of traps.

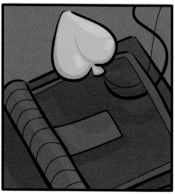

The locket is lost...

but Despereaux lands safely!

...n the coliseum...

Well done, Roscuro.

Come, my friend. Look at your handiwork.

Roscuro watches as Pea is rolled into the arena.

Despereaux runs to the king's chamber.

Sire! Your daughter is in danger!

Your Highness! Please, sir!

But the king doesn't hear. He just continues playing his sad song as a tear rolls down his face.

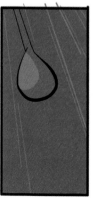

SPLOOSH!

Also lost in his own grief, Lester Tilling opens his front door.

Ah... ahhhhhh....

Dad! Dad! Listen, you've got to help me.

B-b-but y-y-you're dead.

No! No, I'm not!

Now, listen! The princess is in danger!

You're de-de-dead.

BAM!

Dad! Dad! Wake up, please!

Despereaux runs out of the house to search for help and runs straight into...

Furlough!

You're de-de-dead.

Listen! The princess is in danger! She's locked in the dungeon!

Oh, my God!

You're DEEEEAAAAD!

Looking about in despair, Despereaux sees his only chance to find help.

The bell tower!

CLANG!

CLANG!

The bell rings out, but nobody seems to hear. No mouse, anyway.

CLANG!

CLANG!

Within the silent kitchen, André is lost in a deep sleep. But a distant noise invades his dreams.

CLANG!

Oh!

André had dreamed of a bell ringing, calling all the townspeople to a great feast.

André looks around his cold and empty kitchen. Suddenly, he stands up.

Enough!

Dizzyingly fast, André chops an onion, several tomatoes, and, of course, some garlic, all of which he dumps into a gleaming pot.

Ha, ha, ha! Yes!

Mmm!

A beautiful, fragrant steam begins to rise from the kitchen.

On a street nearby, a villager smells something in the air.

More incredibly, he feels a drop of rain. Rain? Is it? Could it be?

POOF!

Look at you! You're still brewing tea!

Boldo!

It's so great to see you!

Would you look at that!

Oh, my! Rain!

Despereaux can smell the aroma, too, and he knows where he must go for help.

Despereaux turns and sees a needle lying on the kitchen floor. He has an idea.

OWWW!

And a talking mouse, too!

Climbing up onto the table, Despereaux tries to make the chef understand.

Listen, you've got to help me.

The princess is locked in the dungeon.

Don't be silly, my little mouse. The princess is perfectly safe in her—

BOOM!

Oh, my.

Boldo, look! It's—

Boldo? Where are you?

There. That way.

Ha!

Despereaux and Boldo make their way through the dungeon, toward Pea's cell.

Strangely, the door is wide open.

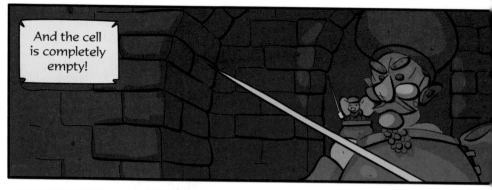

And the cell is completely empty!

But...she was...

Come on, let's go!

Despereaux can make out something advancing toward him.

HURRAH!

Rats!

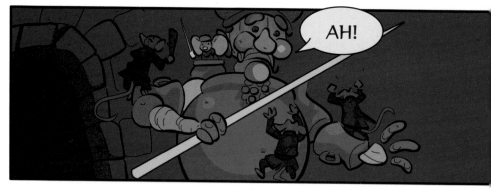

AH!

Meanwhile, Gregory makes his rounds through the dungeon....

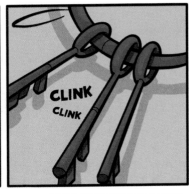

CLINK

CLINK

I'mmm in heeere!

Hearing a muffled call for help, he looks into the cell...

and recognizes a heart-shaped birthmark that could belong to only one person—

his princess.

Gor, what took you so long? I been screamin' in here for hours.

In the streets of Dor, the villagers stare at the sky in disbelief...

as it begins to lighten!

As the king watches his people from the castle window, something seems to change within him.

A flicker of life returns to his eyes.

In the dungeon, Despereaux lies still after his fall.

Little mouse....

Wake up, my brave little friend!

Chivalry. Bravery. Honor.

The princess is in there!

In the
oliseum…

This honor
is all yours, my
friend.

Ring the gong,
and let the feast
begin!

EAT! EAT!
EAT!

Okay, remember when we
id that grief was the strongest
thing a person could feel?

Well, it isn't.

It's forgiveness.

ecause a single act of forgiveness
can change everything.

EAT! EAT!

No.

113

Arriving just as the rats swarm Pea, Despereaux searches for a way to save her.

The cat cage!

High above is the winch that opens the cage...

Gasp!

CREEEEAAAKKK!

MMMMFFF!

He lets the furious beast loose!

116

Cornered, Despereaux backs into the winch...

BUMP!

WHIRRR!

and sends them all hurtling!

AHHH!

Pulling himself up, Despereaux finds he is not alone.

If it isn't our brave little knight. And it seems he came just in time for dinner.

Hmmm. I wonder, should I finish you off myself...

or turn you into cat food?

Suddenly, Roscuro has an idea. He grabs Botticelli's magnifying glass...

and angles it toward a ray of light.

The bright light shines directly on Botticelli!

GYAHH!

Nooo!

Ooooh.

Ah! Please. Nice kitty. No! No!

No!

With the coliseum free of rats and full of light, Despereaux is able to untie Pea.

Thank you, my good gentleman.

Roscuro slowly approaches Despereaux and Pea.

I am sorry.

You have nothing to be sorry about.

A smile breaks across Roscuro's face as a weight lifts from his heart.

Turning away from the window, the king smiles as he looks across the room at the queen's portrait.

So, you could call all of this a big misunderstanding if you wanted to. A king was hurt, so he hurt a rat. And a rat was hurt, so he hurt a princess....

And a princess was hurt...

so she hurt a servant girl without even meaning to do it....

And that servant had been hurting for so long that almost nothing could make her feel better.

But was it a mistake? Or was it just good luck?

Because the servant girl went back to her farm.

And the jailer finally found his princess.

And the king found something stronger than grief.

And the mice finally got rid of their fear.

Ha, ha!

Good one, son!

SNAP!